ROLL UP YOUR SLEEVES AND SAY BYE TO BURN OUT

ROLL UP YOUR SLEEVES AND SAY BYE TO BURN OUT

Dilip Kumar Ojha

GYAN

ISBN: 978-81-212-1215-1

Price: ₹ 140

First Published 2014

Published by

Gyan Publishing House

23, Main Ansari Road

Daryaganj, New Delhi-110002

Phones: 23282060, 23261060

Fax : 91-11-23285914

E-mail: books@gyanbooks.com

Laser Typesetting : Awadhesh Computers, Delhi

Printed at: G. Print Process, Delhi

Cataloging in Publication Data–DK

Courtesy: D.K. Agencies (P) Ltd <docinfo@dkagencies.com>

Ojha, Dilip Kumar.

Roll up your sleeves and say bye to burn out / Dilip Kumar Ojha.

p. cm.

ISBN 9788121212151

1. Self-actualization (Psychology) 2. Success. I. Title.

DDC 158.1 23

OM SAI RAM

Dedication

I dedicate this book to my loving mother and father. They supported me and made me what I am today. They have taught me to respect and love other. I want to give my whole credit to my parents who have supported me in writing my first book.

My mother and father are priceless like a diamond. I sincerely thank my father (H.K. Ojha) and my mother (Kamla Devi).

Contents

Preface

Time has come so ripe to tell you that only a handful of people are lucky enough to live a prosperous life while others are still struggling and accepting whatever fate brings them.

They do not want to put their act together and just want to live with their shortcomings and failure.

This book is a tool for success, it will help you to mould yourself, step-by-step. It will help you to understand the inner strength and to love yourself. This book will help you to come out of the cloud of cuckooland, you have to change your life and fight for it. Roll up your sleeves and then go ahead, never accept poverty which is the free gift of nature. You have to detach yourself from the past and must create and cultivate habits of the rich, you should learn to visualise yourself as a rich man. Bodycells will resonate whenever you come across your goal, you will get attracted towards it. Try to follow the recipe of the successful people.

After reading this book, roll up your sleeves and say bye to burn out, remember until and unless you step out and sweat it out nothing is going to change.

Dilip Kumar Ojha

Preface

Acknowledgements

I want to give my whole credit to my family, they were behind me in pushing my best foot forward. I want to thank them from the core of my heart for their contribution. I thank my friends for sharing their knowledge, and helping me to complete this book. I have taken out the information from the newspapers, books, internet, and from my parents. Last but not the least I thank my wife (Anju).

Dilip Kumar Ojha

1

Introduction

There are many books available in the market which give us the idea of burn out. According to me only a handful of people have understood the real meaning of burn out. If we start fabricating reasons for burn out our mind will start fabricating thousands of reasons.

If we take an honest look then we will come to know that it is a feeling of tiredness, getting frustrated, boredom, becoming less vibrant and less energetic some people feel burn out when they do not get a good job. At times they feel exhausted when they do not get promotion or good salary. There are sections of people who get depressed for not getting acknowledgement in his group or at his work place.

Some people feel burn out because they are one trick pony. I mean they can handle one type of work. They can do one type of work. They have knowledge of one type of work. On the other hand there are a group of people who are jack of all trade but still are not happy.

There are people who want somebody to stand behind them for each and every suggestion; which is not possible we have to become that somebody and take the steps.

Some people get discouraged when they do not get result fast and in an easy way. In the Long run the negative thought get accrued and finally they become a negative thinker. They love to count their failure instead of blessing. In return the negative thought act as a poison, which slowly kills their instinct belief. Some people never have a habit of setting a realistic goal and they suffer ten times with their ambiguous goal. You have to put your leg in others shoes and think from his point of view before coming to the conclusion or else you will end up finding out the real reasons of frustration.

I would like to tell all the readers that we can also live a happy and prosperous life through success and achievement. At this juncture what is needed is to mould ourselves properly step-by-step to come out from the free gift of poverty, which people are accepting naturally. We have to learn to fight. We have to change our self. Our life is not going to change unless we take a few steps forward properly in a planned manner.

2

Find out your Strength and Limitation

Time has come so ripe to tell you that it is necessary to find out our strength and limitation. Find out who we really are. Keeping in mind your strength try to focus on the limitation and if possible try to strengthen. You know yourself better that anybody else. If you know you are doing the right thing then just relax and perform. Many people will try to pull you down because they do not want you to be success. Everyone has a potential but everyone has different potential you shouldn't compare yourself with others. Before giving respect to others, you should learn to give respect to yourself. You should never underestimate yourself. Be sincere there should be no confusion between what you practice and what you preach.

If you have a habit of listening to feedback then you have a hidden strength. Try to make use of it. Feedback will help you in your development and growth. Frankly speaking you must know how to give feedback, focus on the issue, tackle the problem I mean you should focus on the solution. Try to build a mutual relationship. Try to talk with everyone but learn to keep some distance. Everyone has positive and some negative characters. Allow the positive things to get imbibed within yourself. If you want to increase the level of your strength you should make a good circle they will help you, motivate you and encourage you. The pain of growth is temporary but the pain of regret is permanent. Allow your strength to grow. Everyone has their own way of thinking. Some people work for money and for some people money works for them. Some people wait for the customer before filling the shops. Some people fill their shop, decorate and then customers automatically come to them. It is your strength which plays a pivotal role in your life, none other things will come handy to you.

3

Remove your Doubts and Clutters that Annoy you

Some times it is very difficult to balance between life and work. You have to plan everything in advance or else you will get burn out. It is not possible to please your boss and your family. If you want to please your boss you have to go early and come late. If you want to please your family you will have to go late and come early which is not possible. Remove your doubt and clutter from your mind which frustrate you or else good ideas can't get through. You will feel lighter, charged and energetic. Don't get locked in your trivial matter, keep your mind free and allow new things to come. You may feel overwhelmed by the size of your mental and emotional clutter but ensure yourself and do whatever you can to create space in your mind by removing or cleaning all the unwanted doubts and problems that is burning you internally and externally. If you allow them to accrue it will become irritable and you will have to carry where you go, and a day will come you will get burn out. Some times doubt and clutter act as brake with your brake on you can't move further, if you try to do so forcively or rideroughshod on it, you will get burn out. It will drain your energy. Many people have a habit of procrastination. I mean they love to postpone. Many people give excuses of lack of time. There may be many other reasons which are holding him back. It can be a fear of failure, fear of making mistake and fear of risk. Sometimes it can be a friend or foe. First you find out how procrastination can be a friend through intuition. Find out the underlying source of fear and reflect upon it.

4

Do not Miss your Opportunity

Opportunity comes only once you should be ready to catch the opportunity. Opportunity will never come neatly folded to you. You have to catch the opportunity. It is difficult to recognise opportunity. It doesn't mean that opportunity will be a shortcut. Some people try to find out a happy life using shortcut, ill advised and manipulative practices. Many people want to do things over a weekend. Some times obstacle can be an opportunity in disguise. You cannot wait for the obstacle to get cleared off. We have to overcome the obstacle. The more and more obstacle you come across the more closer you are to your dream. If you will take seriously the opportunity then you can overcome. If you will take half heartedly the opportunity then you can't overcome. If you will take full heartedly then you can easily overcome the obstacle. Whenever you come across any obstacle you should be internally controlled and should not be externally controlled. You have to inculcate a positive way of thinking. Always think that you can do. I see many people becoming reluctant when the opportunity approaches and then they feel sorry when they miss the opportunity.

5

Wastage of Energy

Suppose you are going for an outing and you have no plan then you can get down anywhere. You do not have to find out the bus and you do not have to find out the address. You can go anywhere. Throughout the journey you will waste your energy, if there is no goal or no plan. You will end up playing football in the field with no goal post however talented you may be in your game, it will be a wastage of your effort. If your mother is cooking food and if she doesn't know the number of people to be served then either there will be a wastage of food or shortage of food. If there is a shooting competition and if there is no target then you will feel burn out. If you are undergoing some training course and you have no plan then you can stop it after one week or after one month. You have to find out the direction before using your energy.

6

Hidden Energy

Our brain has a lot of untapped latent energy. We should know to utilize it. Suppose you are attending a meeting and after some time you are asked to say something. Exerting all your pressure you braced yourself to say something but due to stage fear or let's say for some other problem. You couldn't speak. You feel like coming back to your seat. You are disgusted, suppose at that juncture, if somebody whispers you that for every five minutes speech you will be paid ten times. Some how you manage to give speech. This shows that we all have energy hidden in our mind.

Suppose you are holding a glass of milk for sometime then your capacity to hold the glass is reduced. It doesn't mean that you are adding something or making it heavy. You just feel tired. It is a human tendency to feel tired or get tired even if you have latent energy but still you are not able to recognize when some body offers you ₹ 1000 for every extra minute you hold, then you might try to hold, it further.

We shouldn't give up easily. If you are tired you should remember you still have energy even if you are mentally or physically shattered remember you still have energy. You can come up.

7

Do not be Reluctant to Set a Goal

You should take out your precious time to write down your goal on papers. In today's world no one has time. Everyone is busy. Everyday thousands of thoughts keep fluctuating in our mind. It becomes difficult to stay focus on anything, you must focus and prioritise those things that will lead to your goal.

When you set a goal your mind gets focus on smarter choices. It will keep you alert. There will be no hotch potch in your mind. You can utilize yourself precisely. Everyone has their own way of setting a goal. I would like to tell you that short term goal is the best option when you reach one goal, you should go for another reasonable goal, and make a picture of the end in mind. Move slowly and you will get confidence as you move further do not allow yourself to get distracted from your goal. Find out fuel from your failure. Failure is the pillar of success, you shouldn't get hurt by fear of failure. You should take failure as an obstacle which you have to overcome. The greatest inventions in the world had hundreds of failure. We should learn something from this.

8

Dead Line, Plan Action

You must have a deadline for everything, when you keep a deadline your mind will remain focused or else you will not be able to concentrate. If you want 10 chairs then go and talk to the carpenter. He would think for a while and then he may ask you to come on some designated day. That day for him is a deadline only deadline alone will not help you. You have to make plan. You have to be smart enough in making plan. Your plan should be specific and must be measurable and Manageable. Your Plan should be achievable and should be realistic. Your Plan should be time bound. You have to take action, unless you take action your ideas will get buried. Without action nothing can be done. You will keep waiting for the day to come, but remember unless you take action nothing will work out.

You have to develop a habit of taking action. Action cures fear. Everyone has a fear, but the moment you take action your fear will be no more. Successful are very active they act upon their ideas and never post pone it. When you act upon your ideas and get it done you get confidence. You feel more secure and build your self reliance. Never wait for the perfect set of condition. The test of a successful people lies in their ability to handle difficulties when they come. Suppose you have bought a new car; You do not want to go for a drive and feel that your car will get hit by other vehicle and feel that there might be a traffic snarl or sometimes the feeling of breakdown of your car comes to you. If you have this sort of feeling you will never have the gut to take action. You should learn to encounter as it comes. You should be ready to confront it as it comes. If your first job is marketing or sales executive then you must be knowing how tough it is. Some times you build strength and try to brace yourself. You may travel at moderate speed around the neigh bourhood to cure fear. Sometimes they drink extra coffee to gain strength to knock at the first door. Action is the cure of all fear.

9

Be True to Yourself

You should be true to yourself. You have to be strict to yourself. No matter you are staying alone or with your parents. You should stay away from bad habits. When you are with your parents. They will not let you do as you wish every time they will keep a tab on you. They will monitor you. They may keep a constant eye on you. The problem comes when you are alone. This is the time for an acid test for you. You have to be self disciplined, without self discipline you will end up no where. When you are strict with yourself your life will move according to you. When you are strict with yourself you know which book to read, and what is right and wrong. You inculcate a habit of doing wise thing. If you will develop a habit of selecting the right things then you will control your life. One day you will see yourself doing things what you like to do and should be done.

If you will not be strict to yourself you will be fooled yourself. If you have a habit of fooling your parents, teachers or friends. I would like to tell you that you are cheating your life, and fooling yourself. The pain of regret will be permanent. Come on the right track, pick up the right things, read good books and mingle with good people. Follow the recipe of good people one day you will get success in your life.

10

Do not Blame or Make False Excuses

Many people have a habit of putting the blame on others for not achieving. Sometimes they label their son as an obtuse. I mean he is slow to understand, less intelligent and less observant. Wherever little bit thinking is required he is unable to think. If you implant the seed of inferiority complex, less intelligent and lack of memory they grow with your age. Some people in order to put some weight on their excuses. They refer it as a congenital problem. We know very well there is no connection of congenital. Congenital problem starts during the period of gestation or at the time of birth. Suppose you have a joined fingers or anything else which is existing from birth, then we can call it a congenital problem.

Let me write another common excuses which we often hear for not getting what he or she wants. Some people love to stay in the college, they love to add degree after degree but they are reluctant to look for job. When the parents force him to do job he would often fall sick the explaination he will give you will be as clear as mud. According to some people someone might have put a hex on him. Sometimes the explanation you will get might look credible. These are rubbish excuses. You should work hard. You should try for job, sometimes it may not have worked out as you had anticipated. Does it mean you will start making excuses or blame others. Some parents do not allow their children to send out of station for their studies. Some people have taken it for granted, if he or she would go in this or that direction then it will be a sign of portent for them. According to them something bad might happen. Something bad is likely to happen. There is a possibility of something bad to happen. These are all rubbish excuses.

A boy was going for on interview and on the way he saw a black cat crossing the road, and he came back home and the explanation he gave was unbelievable. According to him the last minute crossing of a black cat is a sign of portent. You should come out from all these beliefs.

11

Proactive Behaviour Depends on Decision

It means as a human being we are responsible for our own lives, our behaviour is a function of our decision not our conditions. We can give less important to feeling and should be value driven. We have the initiative and responsibility to make things happen. If we carefully look at the word responsibility it is nothing but the ability to choose your response. You shouldn't blame circumstances and condition. Your behaviour should be a product of your own conscious choice based on value rather than a product of their condition based on feeling.

You should be internally controlled. Some people are externally controlled. Some people feel good when the weather is good and if the weather is not good they feel bad it affects their performance. You should not be affected by the weather and the social environment, you should carry your own weather you should develop a habit of asking how can I do it. 'When you say, how can I do it you are asking yourself to find out some alternative and your mind will work. If you say I can't do it your mind stops working. You have to control your *feeling*. You have to choose an alternative or you say a different approach. Always go for *I will attitude* don't say I can't or if only. These are all excuses which will stop you.

12

Object of Derision

If you have ever been an object of derision you would never feel like recalling it with fondness. No body after all likes to be laughed at.

You would feel like recriminating him but for that you have to become on object of accusation. The best thing is to find out your forte I mean your strong point. All of us have something we do well and concentrate on it, forget about your foible. Don't worry about your perfection. You just do it honestly and just wait and watch a day will come when all those who had made fun of you will come to you and you will get eulogy from them. You will get praise or speech in writing.

If you have ever been for a lunch with your boss and after finishing the lunch the waiter comes to you and asks you to pick up the tab and you get shocked because you had never thought that you will have to foot the bill. You feel bad. Sometimes you feel ambivalent whether to pick up the tab or to leave it and get a mixed feeling of attraction as well as repulsion. You like your boss as well as you hate him for not paying the bill. You should never feel embarrassed and should gracefully say no to him and do not feel bad about it. You should not get hurt. He might be oblivious. He might be preoccupied, some people are so self centered and oblivious of the feelings of others and their circumstance.

13

Keep Your Cool and Take a Break

Keep your cool no matter whatever emergency arises at work, suppose you are going with your brother and unfortunately he meets with an accident. At that time you should keep your mind very cool and take the right decision and ask the commuters or the local passer by for the nearest hospital or the taxi driver to take you to the hospital. You have to handle him I mean if you lose your coolness you will not, be able to help him. Many people lose their temper at the slightest irritation. At times we scream at the pillion rider or the driver who is driving slowly in front of us or has forgotten to show the indicator. If you practice the habit of losing your temper on a fairly regular basis. You will get short tempered and it will get locked into your memory if this happens then you will loss your temper for each and every small thing. You will not be able to live a happy life. You will not have a good relation with your spouse and the bad effect of this will hamper the life of your children.

A single word can spoil your friendship and a single word can make your friendship. Whenever you talk with your friends try to select a good word that has a pack of punch, so that you do not have to worry about the extra word to carry the message but remember that words should be kind necessary and truthful. If it is then you can use it. When you get bogged down you should take a break. If you are financially strong you should go for an outing with your family. You can select any hill station, get charged up and rejuvenated. If you are not financially strong you can go for a movie or to a hotel. I mean leave all your office work. Come down to ground. If you want to relax even without going out then in that case you can visualise yourself enjoying near a beach having fun with your friends.

14

Different Perspective

Everyone has a different perspective. I mean they have a different view for everything. Some people think that electric bill should be cleared before the due date. Some people think that electric bill should be cleared after the due date.

Some people wait for the customer before filling their shop and decorating them. Some people never wait for the customer they start packing and decorating the shop, some people wait for the right time to do things. Some people never wait for the right time. Some people work for money and for some people money works for them. Some people want to have their own business. Some people want to work for others business. Some people love to mingle with everyone some people love to stay reserve. Some people love to copy others where as some people love to be copied by others. Some people like to imitate where as some people love to emulate others. Some people love to live a spend thrift life where as some people love to live a frugal life. Some people love to take care of their old family members. Some people leave them to fend for themselves. Some people are maverick. I mean they make their own rules. Some people love to follow the rules.

15

Never Underprice Yourself

You should never think low about yourself. If you will think then you will become. You should visualize to be a rich man one day your visualization will come true. If you think yourself to be inferior then no doubt others will take it for granted. If you think that you are an important person then wear good dress and wear goggles others will also accept you to be an important person. You should dress right. Suppose if you have an examination today then you should get up in the morning refresh yourself, take good breakfast, shine your shoes and put on good dress. By doing this you will get more confidence. Some people love to buy dress after the exam. If you go down to south they buy new dress before the exam. It leaves a big impact of appearance on others. Many times we hear that first impression is the last impression. It is true your presentation should be good. If you put on good dress and if you board a bus or train you will get little bit more respect than others. Give respect to your work. Always consider your work to be important. If you will consider your work to be important then others will start thinking seriously about your work. Never Lament your mistake, knowing that too much regret is also a blunder. Do not worry about trivial matter. Speak like a successful person. Dress like a successful person. It is in your hand if you think you are small then you will become small. If you think you are big then one day you will become. By Law of attraction you should visualise that you are rich and you will become rich. You should visualise. Only positive result then positive result will come to you. Do not allow negative thought to come. You should keep a list of thought changer which can change your negative thought into positive.

16

Build Self-confidence

1. ***What makes you uncomfortable***

   You must find out all those areas where you feel bad, or inferior. Jot down in a piece of paper and try to rectify by creating a positive feeling.

2. ***Share with your friends and your family***

   Roll up your sleeve and try to find out the main cause of it. All issue may not be rectified at least you can check which all issue are presently creating problem to you. Try to get rid of it sometimes you may need to accept it.

3. ***Spring back from your Error***

   Never take your mistake to your heart. No one is perfect. It keeps changing as it is an uphill journey with lots of pot hole here and there.

4. ***Identify your Forte***

   Everyone is good at something. Give credit to your success. Everyone has a different talent and potential. Do not allow yourself to be victimised.

5. ***Count your blessing and Appreciate***

   We are not happy of whatever we have got. You should learn to count your happiness and be satisfied of whatever you have. Never inculcate a habit of not having enough.

6. ***Always have a feeling of happiness***

   Even if you are not feeling happy. You should learn to feel happy Do not allow others to feel low about you. You should respect yourself and others will respect you.

7. ***Pep talk***

   You should talk with yourself that you are rich brave and have the ability to do. In the long run you might feel confident.

17

Personality

We cannot improve our personality in one day or from one class or by reading book. It depends on our father, mother our family back ground.

Presentation: We should focus on our presentation. If our presentation is good then we will get respect and confidence.

Etiquette: It is nothing but manner we cannot change in one day or from one class. It also depends on our parents.

Responsible: You will get responsibility only when others feel that you can do. You should take seriously the responsibility you already have. If you get extra responsibility you shouldn't hesitate. It is a plus point for you.

Optimistic : You should think positive. Count your blessing not your failure. If you will think positive, you will get more positive result. If you allow your positive thought to change into frequency that frequency will bring more positive thought to you.

Negative thought: You should not allow negative thought to come.... Allow only positive thought. It depends on your feeling, if you are feeling positive then positive thoughts are going on. If you are feeling bad some negative thoughts are going on.

Anger: You should control your anger. Anger is one letter short of danger, you shouldn't fight on small topic.

Listen for feedback: Nobody likes to listen for feedback. Some people think feedback means discussion on problem, discussion on mistake. There are two types of feedback positive and negative feedback.

Intelligent: You should read newspaper articles. I mean you should keep abreast of the latest information. You will be able to switch on to some other topic. If one topic is running out of steam.

Trustworthy: You should be honest but you shouldn't be 100 per cent honest. If you are 100 per cent honest then any one can fool and stop you.

Yin Yang: You should know how to talk with a female and how much distance you should keep. If you are a girl you should be womanish. If you are a male you shouldn't be effeminate. If refers to a person who is a boy but he talks like a girl walks like a girl.

There are some more simple points which will help you to improve your personality.

First point is find out who you are. You should help others whenever it is possible. Always be yourself do not put in airs. You cannot put a mask for a long time. You will get exposed one day.

You should keep a congenial atmosphere with your friends and do not keep a dog in the manger attitude. If you have and if you are not using it then you can share.

A thoughtless statement can precipitate an argument, or we can say a thought less statement can eventually lead to an argument, politics, is a hot bed of precipitate. They bring about suddenly new ideas with premature thought and action.

18

Get Rid of Ego

It is better to give up your ego than to suffer later in life. Giving up ego is tough, but once you come out you will be more energetic and vibrant. Stop talking about yourself all the time and try to listen others. He thinks very highly of himself and is very dogmatic. It is a feeling of one's superiority over the others.

It is easy to reach on the top but if your ego is with you then it is very difficult to maintain at the top. Ego is assumption of self importance.

People who have ego never have a habit of asking forgiveness and they never admit whenever they are wrong and they talk too much about themselves. They love to play blame game. If you are really qualified, then work according to the principles, give respect to others never give unsolicited advice. Avoid insinuation.

Excessive prideness is the main enemy of achievment.

If you really want to come out of your ego then do not defend yourself. Listen to others rather than talking about yourself. Bless those who put a hex on you Ask forgiveness and give importance to others.

19

Stop Worrying What Others Think of You

If you know you are on the right track then no need to worry about others. Try to build good habit. If you make good habit and if you practice it everyday then you will become successful. Whenever you have time you should crack jokes with your friend and if you are not good at humour then leave it.

If you think you can do it then just do it. Always have a firm believe in yourself and your work. Many people think that it is very difficult to get success in life. If you want to live a good life you have to be physically and mentally strong. Your health, communication and positive attitude all play a pivotal role in shaping your future. Always try to have a big dream. I mean dream big and act accordingly. Put your ego aside and make friends who know more than you and will help you in your dream.

Find out who is controlling you. You are controlling yourself. Always think that you have every thing to become successful. You shouldn't think that you are deprived of anything. You should select the right response. You can take new challenges, and learn to handle the criticism. Self esteem, should be strong. It will allow you to control your Life. Self respect is very important. How you respect yourself and accordingly it has an impact on your life.

How are you evaluating yourself? If your self esteem is high your risk taking ability will increase and will be ready to accept responsibility. You are open to new opportunities and challenge. You are broad minded person. You never make excuses. You never break the promises you make. So never think about others what they think of you.

20

Soft Skills Can Make or Break Your Career

If you take an honest look and if you think pragmatically then you will see that everything has changed. All rules for success have changed. There was a time when soft skills were not considered as important as technical knowledge skill. There was a time when technical skill knowledge were the only key drivers of career growth and success. Now a days soft skills have become very important and have enough power to make or break your career.

There are people with high technical knowledge and have even reached the top level. A day will come when your graph of success will start declining due to lack of social communication and relationship building skills to manage their work. We can learn soft skills by interacting with our family, friends and the society. As we grow and mature our soft skills get sharpened. Soft skills cannot be learnt in one day or from a book or from any training centre.

Technical skills are must but not sufficient. You need to become a proactive. Planning is necessary but execution is also important. Soft skills can help you to deal with people.

Negotiation skills	:	Language
Interpersonal skills	:	Social grace

Attitude	:	Communication
Motivation	:	Friendliness
Time management	:	Personal habit

Technical abilities are very important but when it comes to climb on a ladder only personality will help you. There are many companies where they have to deal with the customer face to face, only soft skills will be helpful. Soft skills play a vital role for professional success. It cannot be denied in this age of information.

You may get hired for skills and fired for lack of soft skills. Soft skills can give a definite direction to your career. Soft skills are personal quality that increases an individual's interaction. It is often said that technical skills will get you an interview but your soft skills will help to get the job.

It is easier to mould a child then to unmould an adult.

21

Fire Task Earth Task Air Task

Fire Task: Fire task makes quick work of keeping up with your to do list. Fire task will keep you focused on what you need to do today. Fire task can be those task with due date. Next task are task that have no due date elements of fire represent the creative spark in us. Those task which produces something unique. Any inspirational dynamic or productive work such as developing new ideas working on project and taking risk. Without fire task life is repetitive.

Earth Task : The earth element represent the source from which we obtain our nourishment. Earth task are those tasks in our life that have to be done like sleeping, eating and other needs.

Air Task : Any activity that involves thinking. Non doing work activity like goal setting, planning, decision taking, and creative thinking.

22

Humility

It is a common characteristic of great leaders.

Not arrogant or prideful.

Showing submissive respect.

Showing meek or obedient respect.

Unpretentious.

Humility is a state of being humble. Lack of false pride indicate the first test of truly great man. Humility alone can bring happiness.

If there is anything which can carry the burden of unsuccessful organisation or a troubled society is great leadership. Leaders who are humble never say I they say we. They think about team A true leader is known not for his own capability but for his ability to bring out the best in others.

It is hard to become humble. Learning to be humble is of paramount importance.

First thing is to evaluate and understand your limitation. Recognising our limitation doesn't mean giving up new things.

Practice gentleness and be ready to help others without keeping in mind of getting anything from him. Try to, learn something from your seniours.

Always be ready to learn something new. You should never become complacent. You should think that you do not know as much as you think you do. You never know how some one can be of service to you no matter how they initially appear. Try to recall the story of the lion and the mouse.

It is a quality that not many possess. You should degrade yourself. You should cut one's ego down to size. A humble person thinks he should be better than he is.

23

Five Big Leadership Factors

Neuroticism

It is the display of negative emotion such as anxiety, anger, guilt depressed mood. They also have some phobia depression. It relates to irrational thinking poor impulse control. They respond more poorly to environmental stress and are more likely to interpret ordinary situation as threating. They have more depressed mood frequently.

Extraversion

It refers to positive outlook and energetic approach. It refers to people who talks often and are being full of life. They are more involved in social situation. They are more cheerful. They are more engaged with the outside world. This type of person is more likely to be the centre of a group of friends.

Openness

It involves active imagination attentiveness to inner feeling and intellectual curiosity. It relates with intelligence and creativity. They are broad minded. Openness refers unobstructed entrance. Accessible to all not restricted and free from limitation; they are always willing and ready to receive.

Agreeableness

It describes the tendency to conform and concur with others even at the cost of one's own interest and priorities. These people are kind, sympathetic, cooperative, warm and considerate. Those who score high on this facet generally believe others intention to be benevolent.

Conscientiousness

It is a desire to do task well. They are careful and vigilant. They are hard working and reliable. They are more goal oriented. People who have conscientiousness are more organised and less cluttered in their houses. They love to keep things in an apple pie order. They keep the books properly and keep their clothes neatly folded. In other words he is a careful and hard working.

24

Silence Can Refuel Our Mind

Silence has also energy. It will help to focus inwards and allow your true self to speak. During the time of argument you have to control your silence. Just look at him and keep mum. If any where gossiping is going on try to remain silence. Millions of people follow a quotidian schedule of catching train and buses. Very often we are surrounded by noise. Silence will allow you to build awareness and gives your mind a room for introspection and allow you for a wise choice. You can do your work efficiently. We have become so habituated to noise that wherever we go we hear some kind of noise it may be background music in stores car, etc. When we are alone we also can't sit quietly. We go for our cellphone and play some music. We often get distracted everywhere. At least we can try to sit silently after coming back from office by turning off the T.V., music and just relaxing on a chair. By voluntarily cutting yourself from communication you are totally free from all sort of distraction. When you go for silence you are clearing your mind and gathering your energy for maximise performance. By keeping silent you can discriminate right from wrong. What we people normally do is we fill our life with noise in order to avoid silence. It draws people together because only those who are comfortable with each other can sit without speaking. You should learn to understand silence or else you will not be able to understand words.

25

Side Effects of Workaholism

People have become so much concerned about their job that they do not even take leave. They never feel like taking break. Fear of losing their jobs keeps haunting them. Many young professionals are no longer interested in it. Many people do not even remember the last time they took break. You may be good at your job but there are other people who are waiting for the job. Chances of replaceable are for sure. If you take a break then you are opening a can of worms. You are creating problem yourself. Many people do not have a gut to take leave. They do not even give quality time to their children. Many employees do not even claim their leave. They know very well that if they discuss about leave or increment in their salary they are fouling their own next. Some of them think that if they will work hard at this juncture their future might get secured. Some of them have a fear of losing what they have achieved.

Companies should make it easy for employees to take leave. They should enable employees to step out of the line drawn in the sand and go for a break. This commitment of giving them leave is lacking. It has become very difficult to take leave in multinational company. Some of them create a small scenario a day before taking leave.

You will get charged up after taking break and will bounce back more energetically on your work.

26

Expand Concentration Powers

It has become so difficult to concentrate and finish our work on time. Sometimes we give a lick and promise. Sometimes you do your job without enthusiasm, you hope to complete it later on. You might end up having blunt conversation and you might lose your concentration.

(i) Break Your Work into Manageable One

You should work in small portion so that you are able to concentrate and focus on it. Go for one think at a time. You cannot think about all works. You allow your mind to concentrate and you write other work on a paper; you are free to forget and you can give your undivided attention to one of your work. Forget multi-tasking. You will find it difficult to maintain good concentration if you are thinking of two things at a time. Just focus on a single task at a time. If you are mentally and physically fresh, then do your important task.

(ii) Make a List of Daily and Weekly Task

The simplest way is to write it down. Focus on the task at hand. Carry a small pad and write a bullet form list which is quick and easy to read. You can use high lightner to tick and circle all the important date and works so that you can concentrate and plan accordingly.

(iii) Take Regular Break and Recharge your Brain

Concentrate for some time and then take break. It is better to take a break rather than working with no fresh idea. A three minutes break for every 30 minutes of work is a good guideline. It is hard to concentrate when you are tense. It is important to relax when working on a job that needs extra span of attention.

(iv) Select a Good Environment

Some environment are more conducive. A noisy and disturbing is not going to help you get your work done. Spruce up your work place, switch off your cell phone. Tell your friends not to interrupt you. Put a small message "Busy do not disturb me" still if you are getting problem you can choose a quiet place or an empty cabin.

(v) Exercise

The first thing to increase your concentration is by exercising in the morning. You will feel rejuvenated and ready to take on tough problem. You can go for aerobic exercise, or you can go for a walk or simply stroll in the garden. You try to sweat out impurities.

(vi) You Shouldn't over Eat

Over eating will not help you to concentrate. Take light food. You shouldn't eat in front of the television or else you will end up over eating. You shouldn't buy foods that will cause you to over eat, your memory power will decrease. It can even cause headache and you will not be able to concentrate. There is no magic pill that can help you to increase your concentration. Eating food appropriate to your need is a means of extracting energy.

(vii) Tendency to Procrastinate

We have a habit of putting off a task or project. If you will think that the task is boring now then ask your self whether the same work after procrastination will it be any easier. Simplify the difficult task by breaking them into manageable chunk and do the easy one and then take the difficult one.

27

How to Make a Good Conversation

The first thing which is very important is politeness and simple respect in communication. You must use words which will please them. You should never use rude words. I do not know, I cannot tell, they are offensive. Conversation will be colourless unless everyone participates. It is a game that can be played between two three or more person.

The first thing you should remember is that you must have the same standard of understanding. You must find out the comprehension level of your group. You must find out his or her interest before starting a conversation. You should ask question politely in between. Maintain eye contact and try to listen. If you will listen, then you can identify question to be asked based on his statement. All members of the group must do their bit to establish an atmosphere of appreciation, in difference, disdain, or vanity will mar the conversation. Participation doesn't mean that a person has to say so much and no more even if you add a word or a sentence than also it is ok.

You should focus on your intonation. You should know when to raise your voice and when to bring down your voice. It is the movement of your voice. Maintain a balance outlook. Extreme position may lead to controversial remark. You may encourage others to speak by paraphrasing their statement.

You should try to speak in a natural way. You should select an area in which he is well versed. You have to display empathy by entering into other person's world. It is an ability to put oneself in another's place and see the things from that person point of view. One can be empathetic only when he puts his leg in others shoes. Whatever you say should have the qualities or clarity and accuracy. Eye contact sends strong message steady eye contact indicates interest and positive thought. You should think before you speak. A thoughtless statement can precipitate an argument. A thoughtless statement can eventually lead to an argument and suppose if you make mistake, you should appologise. You should converse you shouldn't use hi fi language. You should know the time of comment. You shouldn't butt into conversation. You should focus on your body language. If your body language is not good then it is a leakage of your personality you should uncover your hidden feeling. You shouldn't feel shy. You should listen for feedback. You should never say "Am I boring you" you should never talk to one person when you are in a group. When one topic is running out of steam. You can switch on to some other topic. You must ask their name and you should use it between the conversation and remember do not forget to introduce yourself. You can get the person to introduce you to someone else.

A conversation is more than an information exchange. To converse you have to show an interest in the other person. Give him or her your full attention.

28

Roll up Your Sleeve

You have to get your act together. You have to get yourself organised and plan in a systematic way and then do it in an effective manner and must come out of the cloud and stop living in 'cloud of cuckoo land'. Don't just assume that your wishes will come true without your sincere effort. You have to be really aware of the real world. You must not have ideas and plans which are unrealistic. You have to be more realistic. You can't just make a killing on any of the ideas. Your ideas must be realistic. There are people who makes money hand over first and are earning lots of money. If you take a deep look then you will see that they are really working more than us. On the other hand there are people who are hand to mouth and hardly earn money. It is in your hand how much to earn. If you just sit on your hands whole day how much work would you able to complete. When you are sitting on one's hand you are doing nothing instead of helping others or yourself you are merely sitting on them... This is the right time to take action and help yourself when no one is willing to help you. When your friends leave you high and dry they desert you in your time of need, you are left to fend for yourself.

You have to think of ways to get out of difficult situation. You must have a good acumen, your mind should be sharp. You have to keep ideas of everything and try to become knowledgeable and develop a habit of taking a very quick decision. You must prepare for hard work. You must roll up your. Sleeves and get the job done. You must gain momentum. You must be humble and solution driven. You must effectively target solution to situation, but not dwelling on it any more than that. You should never be wet blanket. You should never prevents others from enjoying and should never dampens others enthusiasm.

29

Stop Comparing

Most problems in life are due to comparison. Everyone is unique. Everyone has a quality which is different from others. Beauty lies in the beholders eyes that is the beauty of the individual. It is we who have a habit of comparing whenever we see two things at a time. You cannot compare a rose with a lotus they have their own quality and have their own beauty. If you start comparing with others you will end up comparing. The more and more you compare you will end up comparing yourself. You will feel more and more inferior. If you stop comparing you are yourself neither superior nor inferior. Just try to see for a moment without comparing. You can see the real beauty within. You should accept others beauty and never inculcate a habit of playing mischief and start comparing. An egoist thinks about himself. An egoist is not content with himself, Egoist feeds on comparison.

30

Never Hesitate to Love Yourself

Loving yourself is mainly having self respect. Never think that you are living your life for nothing. In order to love some one you must love yourself. Stand in front of a mirror. As you look in the mirror do you focus on the piece of hair that goes its own way, a facial mark, a spot on your shirt or the size of your nose. Are your inner words full of criticism and scan past your valuable features.

For a mentally positive self concept, notice the warmth in your smile, dimple in your chin when you give yourself a pat on the shoulder and some encouragement you are contributing to your own self, esteem.

Treat others with love and respect they will repay you with the same kindness.

If you always focus on your own faults you will most likely highlight the short coming and you will become a negative person.

If you suffer from low self esteem it is possible that the root cause is a case of insufficient self love.

Just like flowers that needs watering to grow. Learn to nurture yourself in everyway. Make a habit of praising yourself. You must have confidence in your abilities. You can also support yourself by visualizing desired outcome.

Love is passionate and active. Each small step an individual takes to replace lies with truth, criticism with praise, fear with love is a step to a new way of living. You cannot enjoy happiness if you are not at piece with yourself. If you lack your own love, then you attract people and circumstances that mirror your negative belief. In order to draw in loving people you have to love yourself first. Our bodies are about 60 per cent water. It depends on individual. Whenever any negative thought comes it get mixed up with the water and whole negative spreads inside our body cells then according to the law of attraction we get more and more negative results.

You can check yourself periodically by checking your feeling. Suppose if you are feeling bad that means you must have said something negative about yourself. You must keep a list of thought changer that can change your negative thought to positive. If you really want to heal your problem then start loving yourself. Accept yourself as you are, do not go for criticism. If you have done any blunder mistake. Never lament your mistake just forgive yourself. Switch your scary thought to a pleasure thought. Criticism breaks down the inner spirit. Praise builds it up. Praise as much as you can.

31

Time Management

"Time management is an oxymoron. You cannot manage time but you can manage yourself".

Nowadays life has become so busy that it has become so difficult to please everyone. You have challenges at home as well as in your office.

You have to plan everything in advance. Self discipline is the key factor. It is not possible to give quantity time. You can give quality time. Make a list of things from the mundane to the critical. You have to highlight your important work. In reality balancing is difficult. Work on small portions everyday so that you can complete before the due date.

Every one has a prime time. You must find out your prime time. You shouldn't compare your primetime with others. Prime time means concentration time, some people can work better in the morning and some can focus more in the evening. Give yourself a time goal to finish your work. After finishing one work you raise the bar and start another one. Many people do not have a habit of delegating the work. You can share your work.

It is important to take a break. If you will stress yourself your body clock will get disturbed your circadian sleep pattern get disturbed. Your appetite may gets disturbed. You may get up in the morning with a little appetite for breakfast and may not eat anything till afternoon there will be a severe consequences on your health. Set up more realistic schedule. Once you understand the actual time of completing you will get motivated "Long term planner use a monthly chart so that you can plan ahead".

You have to balance the conflicting demand of time for study, leisure, earning money and job hunting. You really have to plan everything. You have to prioritise everything. You can do it by setting a clear goal and breaking your goal into discreet steps and reviewing your progress. You can do all these in chart paper so that you can plan ahead.

First you try to follow according to your plan which you have jotted down. Then ask yourself. At what time of day do I do my most effective work. Sometimes we are alert in the morning. Try to keep everything in an apple pie order. You shouldn't mess up your room. You mustn't litter your room if you see every where crumbled pieces of cake lying here and there or stain of tea, or pepsi your mind may not be able to concentrate.

32

Develop Alternative Study Places Free from Distraction to Maximise Concentration

You have to cut down all the distraction which you are likely to face. You cannot do your work in a noisy environment. Your mind will not work. Good ideas will not come to you. You can select an alternative place which is free from distraction so that you can give your best. You can shut off your cell phone. You can even tell your friends not to disturb you.

Clear off the work space and keep what is needed. If your friends keep distracling you, set a time and place to have a break. With so many multi-task in hand avoiding distraction at work is not easy. You have to control your mind and control your environment when you look for alternative place make sure you leave your cellphone behind. You can turn off internet. Start as early as possible before the rest of the world is up.

"First thing in the morning what's ahead for the day, always go to sleep knowing you are prepared for tomorrow."

Before going to bed you take out your precious time and do some planning for the next day so that it will be easy for you to sleep properly, when you get up in the morning you should check your days plan and go ahead.

Some learners need more frequent break for a variety of reasons. More difficult material may also require more frequent break, prioritize assignment when studying, get in the habit of beginning with the most difficult subject or task.

33

Abuse of Time

At the work place abuse of time takes different forms. Doing personal work during officer hours socialising and delaying decision making are some of them. Surprisingly if you check you will be shocked. Most of the time they do others job. Atleast you should learn to say gracefully no. They work to satisfy their individual interests. They handle too many assignment and finally there is little or no output. You should schedule and execute task in a way that it reduces their effort without compromising with the output. If you scrutinize properly then you will see yourself how you spend most of your time in unproductive ways. Planning is very important. Periodically you have to monitor your progress. You have to allot specific time to interact with visitors. You can even delegate some of your less important task to your subordinate.

34

Fall off the Wagon

When you fall off the wagon you go back to drinking alcohol in large quantities after having abstained from it. It refers to the resumption of bad activity.

One of my friend once visited his boss to discuss about the increment of his salary. The boss was not ready to listen to him after insisting repeatedly he gave him no motion I mean he gave him promotion without any increment in his salary. He became ballistic at him, my friend told him about his family problem and other problems. He was not willing to listen. He gave him tongue lashing. He was flipping out at him. He was trying to lead him by the nose at that juncture he felt very bad and was trying to justify him, but indirectly he was fauling his own nest. Then he realised that he was just left to fend for himself. He was very sad and felt very bad about it and then he started his old habits of drinking and smoking. You shouldn't take it to your hurt.

You shouldn't give up. You see when you cut a big tree from the middle you will see after some days or month leaves start sprouting out again. If you will cut it from the middle again after somedays you will see leaves coming out this shows that when the tree is not giving up then why should we give up. We shouldn't bury our ideas. We should implement it. You should learn to fight back.

35

Visualizing is Very Important

You should learn to visualize. Once you start visualizing you will get whatever you are visualizing. Suppose you want to become rich then you have to visualize that you have money. You have to believe that you have. You can do it by keeping a good purse and also keep money little bit more than you normally keep. According to the law of attraction you will experience yourself. You are getting much more than what you were getting earlier.

When you focus everyday or visualize again and again each and every cells get the image of the visualisation and then you vibrate and response with every thing that is in touch with that frequency. Desire must first be created in thoughts and then they are created in real life. You must believe that you have received. You must emit the feeling frequency of having received. Whenever you are visualizing you try to visualize as if you already have. What ever you will focus you will attract. Whenever you see any doubt lingering in your mind or when you feel that how it will happen. If you do so then you are emitting a frequency that contains lack of faith. You must never be doubtful, feel good say I am getting. In our mind our thoughts keep fluctuating, we have to select some of them and focus on them repeatedly. A day will come and you will see yourself your visualization coming true.

The first step is to ask or imagine. You can do it by writing on a piece of paper or keep focusing it every time.

36

Stop Underestimating Your Odds for Success

Underestimating your odd can stop you dead in your tracks. Overestimating your odds can spur you to tackle monumental task and win. If you want to improve your motivation spend less time around negative people and smile at people even when they are rude. Try to mingle with successful people. Read good books. Try to find your odd and work out to improve.

You should talk to those people who have achieved what you are trying to achieve. You always motivate yourself with books, people or groups. It will help you to achieve what ever you are dreaming.

Sometimes we are very close to victory, but at the last minute some odd pulls our rug and we lose.

You should find out chink in armour I mean you should find out his weak point. I mean find out the weak point of your obstacle and then over power it. If you feel the obstacle is big then you will work hard and will put your best foot forward and by doing this you can easily overcome any obstacle no matter whatever may be its size. Never assume you have succeded the odd until you have really over powered. We have different types of odd.

External Odd

These odds are not in your hand such as the economy physical limitations or natural disasters.

Internal odd: These odds are one time issue but you have direct control over them such as debt, cash flow, time availability, or talent.

Habitual odd: These odds can only be removed with behavioral change the harder the odd, the more time it will take to overcome

37

The Magic of Big Dream

It doesn't mean You have to live in cloud of cuckoo land. If you get into the habit of dreaming big then you can really achieve because you have made up your mind. Everyone has a different perspective. Your perspective should be of achieving. It is your choice to dream a big one or a small one you might have a goal that might be difficult to achieve or it may be rather frightening. Many people prefer to take the back foot but you should take the best foot. You should have a strong belief in yourself. You shouldn't settle on small dream. Big dreams will push your limit. You may end up achieving more than you ever thought, because of big dreams so many new inventions have come up and cures for diseases. Big dreams will give you opportunity you should always dream big and reach high. It just might come true. Do not ever be afraid to dream big. You can face any sort of challenge.

Dream big is much more than it is. It is a complete system for conscious vision, growth, and results that work for everyone. You should eliminate your limiting thoughts and belief.

Just believe that you can achieve your dream. Then your mind will find the ways to do. Always try new approaches for your dream. Just ask yourself how to achieve then your mind will work for you and you may get new ideas.

38

Mind Diet

Time is very ripe for us to think big. You have to be environment conscious. The body is what the body is fed. In the same way the mind is what the mind is fed. Mind food is nothing but our habits, attitudes, personality our mind diet makes the mind.

Roll up your sleeves and untie your past and get disconnected from the past. You have to detach from the past. It is not possible to link past with present. If you really want to do something new then you have to forget your past and think about your goal.

Your personality depends on your environment, people, friends, with whom you are in touch. If you keep a very close relation with pessimistic people. You will become a pessimist. If you are in touch with high profile people your level of thinking will go up. If you want to get change in future you will have to change your environment. You should never get judged by inferior negative minded person. People hardly bother about the quality and education of the person before judging. You should select friends who are broadminded. You should mingle in new groups and try to get new ideas. You should select friends who are successful. Do not allow negative thoughts to come it will act as a poison. It will reduce the size of our thinking.

You should always look for new ideas. If you will read newspaper magazines, you will get new ideas Thousands of new ideas are floating we have to pick up. If you take good diet for your mind I mean if your environment is good then you will have a sharp mind and can make a wiser decision. Some more important tips for a healthy mind. You should take a regular exercise. You should treat others as you treat yourself. Try to inculcate the knowledge of common sense. You should stay focused in taking your own decision. Check your conversation some conversation is healthy and you will get motivated some conversation will pull you down. You might get demoralised.

Suppose you are good at skating but if your trainer ignores you. Then you might lose your confidence. You may get totally depressed even if you are good at skating. A word of encouragement will really motivates your inner feeling. A single word of discouragement will demotivate you. Let me write a few food tips for brain. You should never skip meal. You should never never skip breakfast try to have atleast five portions of fruit and vegetables everyday and drink lots of water.

Whenever new ideas come, must write down. Your ideas may sprout any time you shouldn't let ideas escape, or else you are destroying the fruits of your thinking. You can sharpen your ideas.

Take advice from experts, there are many qualified people. We just have to get opinion from them. There is no reason to fear we should think fearlessly. Fearless thinking has its own beauty whenever you are in a good environment sometimes you may get an authentic information. You can implement it.

39

Secret of Success

If A, B, C, D, E, F, G, H, I, J, K, L, M, N, O, P, Q, R, S, T, U, V, W, X, Y, Z is equal to 1, 2, 3, 4, 5, 6, 7, 8, 9, 10, 11, 12, 13, 14, 15, 16, 17, 18, 19, 20, 21, 22, 23, 24, 25, 26.

Now see what is 'HARD WORK' and how much does it weight

H+A+R+D+W+O+R+K= 8+1+18+4+23+15+18+11= 98%

Now see what is knowledge and how much does it weight

K+N+O+W+L+E+D+G+E

11+14+15+23+12+5+4+7+5=86%

Let us see how can we get 100%

ATTITUDE

A+T+T+I+T+U+D+E = 1+20+20+9+20+21+4+5= 100%

OPPORTUNITY

O+P+P+O+R+T+U+N+I+T+Y

15+16+16+15+18+20+21+14+9+20+25=173%

LUCK

L+U+C+K = 12+21+3+11 =47%

LOVE

L+O+V+E = 12+15+22+5=54%

INTELLIGENT

I+N+T+E+L+L+I+G+E+N+T

9+14+20+5+12+9+7+5+14+20=127%

Now we can see if you want to be satisfied with 100 percent. You can select yourself and if you have an insatiable curiousity to get more than 100 percent then you have to check yourself. The area of interest should be precise and narrow. Suppose you have any sort of plan then it is better to work on it instead of telling everyone who ever you meet, they might destroy your plan or they may poison your plan. It is better to make use of the latest technology and keep moving forward. Remember never compromise with a small achievement you should see a big achievement and never give up after facing any obstacle. The more obstacle you overcome the more closer you are towards your objective. If you want 100 per cent result you have to focus on your attitude. Attitude cannot be changed in a day. It develops as we mature. Suppose you are living in an environment where negative people are dominating the positive people then you will also become a pessimist. Attitude normally depends on E factor.

(i) Environment

(ii) Experience

(iii) Education.

Environment

We have to check our environment. We cannot change the place completely. We can select the influences from them. Talk with good people and get good ideas from them. Do not interact with negative minded people. Every children have a different way of receiving their guest some of them will invite politely and others will invite you with no respect. Everything we do starts as a thought. Our thoughts influence how we feel and what we do. If you spend with negative people you can expect to feel bad. If you spend your day with optimistic people then good things will happen to you, positive thinking is extremely natural. Sometimes babies are born in a negative thinking family they absorb the negative impulses and attitude as they grow. The only thing what we can do to develop good attitude is:

- Develop a spirit of positive thinker
- Forgive if you can
- Go for the best
- You are what you think
- Love everybody
- Keep abreast of yourself
- Better coping skills during the times of stress.

You have to be very careful with the people you talk:

- Avoid people who would demotivate you
- Never keep a meeting with a negative outlook
- Try new things with different method
- Filter your thought which will flourish.

You should take out your precious time to think about your visualization once you focus everyday your body cell will resonate when it comes to it. Suppose you want to buy a cellphone and you discuss everyday with your friends, and you are checking the prices then suppose you go to market for some work and if you come across any mobile shop then you will get attracted to that shop it will act like a magnet. So make a good environment. It depends on environment. Social environment refers to the culture created by humans it also involves people whom we interact other than people it also includes their living, working conditions, income level educational background and the communities.

We have to check the way we behave our relationship, education and occupation. We need to step back and look at what kind of environment we have created for ourself and those around us.

Experience

Our attitude changes according to our experience. If you will learn by your own experience it will be a long lasting and provides better learning. If you learn by positive experience. It will become a long lasting. If you will overcome obstacle yourself then you will experience the whole process. If you experience yourself it will help you to identify the mistake yourself. You can even rectify the problem. If you have experience then you can get the opportunity to take some challenging responsibilities. If you have no experience you are unlikely to be successful.

Education

Education is a process of imparting knowledge. If you get good education your attitude will change. If you are educated then you can become a contributing member of society:

- Formal Education
- Informal Education
- Non-formal Education

Formal education is class room based provided by trained teachers. Where as informal educations refers to that type of education which takes place outside the school like library under trees, home. If you talk about class room education there you will not see absentism often they will come everyday and they will have the same teacher every time. Those who are attending outside school they may not be regular their teacher may keep changing.

Non-formal education includes, learn to swim programme community based sports programs N.C.C. Boys Scouts, Girl Guides.

40

Do not Keep Self Interest Behind Friendship

You will come across many types of friends. You shouldn't be in a hurry to make friendship. First you should find out your friend's nature, attitude and behaviour. Never keep a self interest behind friendship. Selfishness destroys friendship. True friendship, takes time. You should not hurt your friend.

You will get many types of friend, but you should know to select. Sometimes you will come across friends who do not want to change their life. They do not want to work hard they are not bothered about rolling up sleeves and to work hard. They are all self satisfied. They are accepting what ever it comes in their life. Now you should take the right decision whether to make friendship with these type of people or not. On the other hand there are other people who have a dog in the manger attitude, they have but will not share with you. Even if they will share they will take it back when you really need it. Trust is required for good friendship. Some friends will come to you as long as you give them pleasure.

Some people are always ready to get their act together. They are hard working. They mingle with everyone. They are ever ready to allow good thoughts to come. They keep their mind open and allow good thoughts to enter. They have an open heart and an open mind and never hesitate to accept good views from people around them. They never bother about the caste. They never discriminate. They are optimistic. They talk about prosperity. They do not have time to criticise about others.

41

Love Your Family

You may get everything but if you do not have a family then you will feel almost hollow every where. You should take out your time and spend some time with your family. At least quality time can be given to them. No doubt you have a busy life quantity time may not be possible.

In this modern age half of the people after getting married they prefer to stay away from their parents. You should never do that because they are the one who have brought you up and now when the time has come for you to take care of them you are quiting your responsibility. Parents have the biggest contribution in children's achievement, success and almost everything. Children learn from their parents, they have a good observing power. They copy every thing and we know very well parents are the role model for their children. If your nature is good and have a good personality children will copy you if you are rude and ride rough shod every time your children will learn the same thing. We should love our parents and never leave them to fend for themselves, if they have problem we should give them all type of help. My family is everything, for me. My wife supports me in everything, I do. My wife loves my parents. My father was in police department he has retired from the post of deputy commandant of police from Mizoram. I have two sons Akash and Prakash I love my family and my family loves me they have motivated me I am very fortunate to have them if you get family support then you can achieve whatever you want. You should never underestimate the support of your family, if your family, is standing behind you then you can overcome any obstacle. Remember learn to give respect to them. You should speak politely to your elders. We should love our parents because they sacrifice a lot for us. They provide us our need emotionally and financially. They are always ready to accept us regardless of what we have and what we don't have. If you disrespect your parents then you will not have true respect for anyone, parents bring up you with great love. Their prime goal is to make their children happy and satisfied. We all know how father works hard to earn money for the children facing multiple problems of day to day life. Though we can never pay back their immense favour atleast we must help them in their need.

Parents are considered next to God we shouldn't disappoint them. If you are disappointing your parents that means you are disappointing your God. There are many parents who are deprived of respect and love. Their children do not give respect to them they always malign them. They use abusive language. They torture them sometimes they kick them out of the house and sometimes they leave them in an isolated place. Please stop all this. Please love your parents. Love your family. We are so busy growing up that we often forget that they are also growing old.

There is a saying that mother and father can love their ten children but ten children cannot look after the two people who created them. We should treat them with love respect and kindness. They help us when we are down their love for us is selfless and boundless. Disobedient and disrespectful children kill their parents before their actual death. They shatter their beautiful dream. They leave their parents in a lurch. They leave them in a difficult situation. Take care of your parents love them and support them. If you will love them then your dream will come true.

42

How to be a Responsible Person

Responsible person can stand up on their own actions you need to prove that you can do it:

- Tackle whatever is in front of you
- Stop making excuses
- Learn from mistake
- Understanding self
- Responsibility to nature
- Social interaction
- Do not put things off
- Be trust worthy
- Take care of your own matter
- Do more than belong: Participate
- Do more than care: Help
- Do more than believe: Practice
- Do more than forgive: Forget
- Do more than dream: Work.

If you want to be a responsible person than follow some of them. If you really want to be a responsible then remember some more points.

Flow with your own nature and allow your subordinate the same freedom. Try to increase your attention span despite your pressing problem. Keep an appointment with yourself at least once in a day. Never lament your mistake knowing that too much regret is also a blunder. Never waste a single moment of your day. Try to learn something from wise and stupid.

Act in a moment thoughtfully and according to the situation.

Mingle with others without losing your identity.

Come down to ground zero after the end of each hectic day. If you really want to be a responsible person then you have to mind your words and language that you use. Words are the tools of thinking. The maximum words you have at your command the clear and more accurate your thinking will be. Words are your medium of exchange. With words you relate to people communicate your feeling and thought you can influence them persuade them and control them. In short with words you shape your destiny. Your words are your personality. The right words in the mouth of a responsible person has quadrupled his business the wrong words used by the campaign orator has lost an election, words have changed the direction of history. Words can also make you a very good responsible person, you can rise from mediocricity to success. If you want to handle your problem like a responsible person. You have to become phlegmatic a phlegmatic individual is someone who doesn't show his emotions, he seldom gets excited or angry about anything since he is not easily upset and remains clam he is the ideal person to have in a crisis. You should never have a mercurial temperament. You will not be able to predict yourself, your mind will keep fluctuating. You will frequently change your opinion.

Our Language is the reflection of our self. We should try to use good language it will tell about your family and the type of environment you have been brought up.

43

Believe in God

We should have faith in god we should believe him unconditionally. Millions of people are following a diurnal schedule of doing their job and are not satisfied with their job and are losing faith in God.

Believe me just have faith in him and leave your problems up to him and do your hardwork. He will handle you and may come in disguise of an obstacle. We people have become self centered and are fully depending on our friends, money but surely not on God.

How can we love God whom we cannot see, when we cannot love man whom we can see. Try to have faith in god you will get blessing. It is like having a computer and knowing its potential but not having a clue how to use it. We know about god and his super natural power but yet we are very reluctant to follow the way our god is asking us to do.

When you interact with people who have faith in god and when you will come to know the experiences they have then your faith in god will increase.

Whenever you get time go to Shirdi, Vaisnodevi and other places unconditionally you will get blessings. Surely you will never come empty hand.

Remember you have to work hard then only god will help you if you will help yourself than god will help you.

44

Spark within Us

You must have seen small children full of happiness. They find happiness in everything. If you give them chocolate they feel happy. If you take them for an outing, they feel happy. The thing is, when we grow up the spark of happiness decreases, it converts into spark of frustration and disappointment. We have to maintain our spark of happiness, and also should help others in finding out their spark of happiness. Most of the time it is our own way of approach. If you constantly strive for something like getting a good job or a good friend which you think will help you in finding your spark of happiness, then just forget it. The truth is after getting your spark of happiness, it will fade when you come back again to your mundane life style.

If you are externally controlled and looking for something which is out of your reach, it might lead you to unhappiness. It is not advisable to think about matters which are beyond your control. Just reframe your thought and count your blessings and the strength. You must always be in touch with your flaming self respect and learn to find your spark of happiness, even if your are sad. No sadness is felt; we feel when our desire is shuffled. If you compare yourself with others then you will see enjoying more on a regular basis and experience less stress than others. Some people feel lack of money is the main reason behind spark of frustration. Just merge in the joy of happiness with your family and friends.

45

Find Out when to Stop

Everyone has a goal to achieve. What is important may not be known by most of us. You should know when to stop and when to start. You must stop to check whether you are on the right track or not.

You shouldn't just keep moving, check the direction of your goal and keep a tab on it. Once you have successfully checked the path, find out all the rough side and the soft side of your journey to success, then move on swiftly.

Patience is the most important quality for nurturing ideas. The distance between idea and result is usually a lengthy process. It doesn't happen overnight and the irony is that many people are reluctant to accept the fact. They do not know when to stop asking. They want instant result, instant gratification, and instant acclaim.

Some people love to accept half baked idea. Never go with your half baked idea. Stop, and accept full baked idea. If you have full baked idea, the best thing is to play close to the vest instead of telling it to everyone. Many full baked ideas are orphaned near birth.

Just find out when to stop as your ideas come floating. We are all infalliable. The worst part is to figure out when your falliability is on display. If anyone is helping you to find out your problem, you should accept it, and never have a notion that he disagrees with you.

If someone argues with you, it doesn't mean he disagrees with you. If he doesn't disagree, it doesn't mean that he agrees with you. Many people come up with a headline ideas but no text. I mean they do not work on it. You should keep some distance from those people who love to rationalize their mistake, learn to stop yourself from mingling with every classic idea people, they love to dream, speculate and fantasize. Go ahead with those types of people who are classic executors. They have a quality of adhesive, tenacity and firmness.

Try to find out the best in your area. Then you tear it apart and check what makes it the best. Then check your performance and try to match it.

46

Tactful Leaders

(i) The law of leadership is to get into the mind first.

(ii) You shouldn't try to be better, but be different.

(iii) The ability to concentrate and to use your time well is everything. No matter whether it is business or anywhere else.

(iv) Tactful leaders know how to handle bad days which are indelible.

(v) Tactful leaders know the difference between strong ego which is essential and large ego which can be destructive.

(vi) Tactful leaders have to be proactive no matter what the weather looks like.

(vii) Tactful leaders know how much to bite and how much they can chew.

(viii) Tactful leaders intelligence causes so much fear or respect that it often overshadows his leadership personality.

(ix) Tactful leaders tell their subordinate what he is going to do; then he does, and once again explains how he did it.

47

The Game of Stalking

You must have seen in the olden days, it took a long training before going for hunting. We all know solitary animals grazing in the forest are safer. I mean big tigers and other animals sometimes leave the solitary animal. The hunters keep themselves slow and move side by side of the horse and when they come close to the animal approaching, they immediately come out and shoot. Sometimes the hunter clothes himself like a pig.

The tiger thinks a pig is coming and ignores it. When the hunter finds the tiger approaching, he comes out and kills. Figuratively speaking, try to make others more comfortable and make them feel more important. If you will give them importance then they will disclose you their secret or you can find out his chink in armour. Never have a feeling that if you pose as a fool you become a fool. In order to get the best information always cloth yourself in such a way that you know nothing about it.

We know the meaning of omen, good luck or bad luck, sometimes we learn more from bad luck rather than good luck. You should get rid of giving justification for all your bad luck.

You can also find out fuel in your bad luck.

You must never inculcate a habit of leading anyone by his nose, and never expect anyone to become your ecochamber. You should give them a feeling of superiority.

It will open an avenue of success. Normally when we stalk someone or something we follow the person or animal very closely without being spotted.

48

Never Get Trapped in a Honey Trap

Your competitors may set up a honey trap to get you to spill the beans. Sometimes they may come with their arm candy or attractive people to entrap, or get information. Some people have a habit of pretending to be unwell. Some people have a habit of making it clear to everyone that they are unhappy. Some people have a habit of concealing a problem or difficulty. Never disclose everything with these types of people. These people sometimes display their insincere rather exaggerated emotions. Instead of making it a private affair they invite a lot of people, but remember you have to be bold enough in your decision and never disclose unnecessarily.

We all must be knowing of hydro electric plant, where water flows and circulates and it generates electricity. In the same way never live in a stagnant environment, come out and feel free and never get trapped under anybody's pressure. You must never feel bounded by anybody.

Honey trapping involves coaxing information. I mean to persuade someone by kindness or flattery to get information. Sometimes honey traps are used to lure victims into compromising situations.

If you are innocent then you will walk away, or else the end result of honey trap can be tragic. You should never be in a hurry to disclose or make friendship with anyone; look for myriad of other excuses.

Pay attention to your surroundings, avoid group of people you do not know, be extra cautious while sharing your ideas with others.

49

Provocative Ideas

This book will help you to perform at your level best. After reading this book you will get distinguished from the crowd. No matter whether you are a school going, college going or a professional, after reading this book, there will be a dramatic change in your personality, behaviour and attitude. This book will help to mitigate your problems which you may be facing on a fairly regular basis. This book will inspire you and will show you a new ray of hope for all those things which had been a problem to you.

Roll up your sleeves and change your perception and get exposed to new things.

(i) Get spiritual. When you will come closer to an answer to some of your life's tough question, you will get more clarity and may feel like handling the situation at your own risk.

(ii) Never accept opinion from others of yourself. You can take feedback, whether it is a positive or negative, but what is more important, is to depend on your own values in making decision.

(iii) Never worry about perfection. If something doesn't work out according to your anticipation, never get frustrated. Just feel good whenever you get to learn new experiences.

(iv) Squash Negative thoughts. Whenever you feel negative thoughts are running, then try to discontinue

the thought, and allow only positive thought. You must keep a tab on your thoughts, try to monitor them, or else it will be the main cause of your slump.

(v) Brain Storming. It is a process for creation of ideas. In this process you can combine different ideas and can continue to build on it. You have to take a deeper look. You must never bogged down on one objective. It is natural that when you hear someone else's solution. You get locked in the solution rather than coming up with their own solutions.

(vi) Never Encourage Ultracrepidarian. You will come across ultracrepidarior who has a habit of giving advice on matters he himself knows nothing about. Take the advice of those who limit his comment to his area of expertise and avoids passing judgement on things he knows nothing about.

You should be aware of those people who are doing the exact opposite of what they normally do. Some people love to go against the grain by trying to be an honest advisor. Stay away from people who are always driven by self-interest. They are normally devious and crafty. Stay away from cunning and sly people.

(vii) Find Out Your Passion. Everyone has a passion. You should find out your passion, and never compare your passion with others. Do yourself a favour and figure it out, it will change everything for you.

(viii) Have a gut to Change. When you know that you are not happy and unsatisfied with your life. You should understand on an emotional level and must have a gut to change yourself. You must have a nerve ending desire to change.

(ix) Re-train your thinking. Living in victory means, sometimes you have to develop new habits.

If you have been negative for a long time, you have got to retrain your thinking from "I can't" to "I can" From "It won't happen" to "It will happen". My best days are still out in front of me. Sometimes you have to wipe out all outdated information and go for something new.